EX LIBRIS
THIS BOOK BELONGS TO

# VOLUME ONE

# VIKING MYTHS

## JACQUELINE MORLEY

Published in Great Britain in MMXVIII by
Scribblers, an imprint of
**The Salariya Book Company Ltd**
25 Marlborough Place,
Brighton BN1 1UB
www.salariya.com

© The Salariya Book Company Ltd
MMXVIII

HB ISBN-13: 978-1-911242-48-2

1 3 5 7 9 8 6 4 2

A CIP catalogue record for this book
is available from the British Library.

Printed and bound in China.

**Illustrations by:**

**Patrick Brooks**
Loki's Children
Rebuilding Asgard's Wall
Idunn's Golden Apples
Frey and Gerda

**Alessandra Fusi**
In The Beginning
The Making Of Asgard
The Marriage Of Njord and Skadi
How Thor Got His Hammer

Visit
# www.salariya.com
for our online catalogue and
**free** fun stuff.

# VIKING MYTHS

## JACQUELINE MORLEY

*Illustrations by:*
Patrick Brooks
Alessandra Fusi

VOLUME ONE

SCRIBBLERS
*a* SALARIYA *imprint*

# CONTENTS

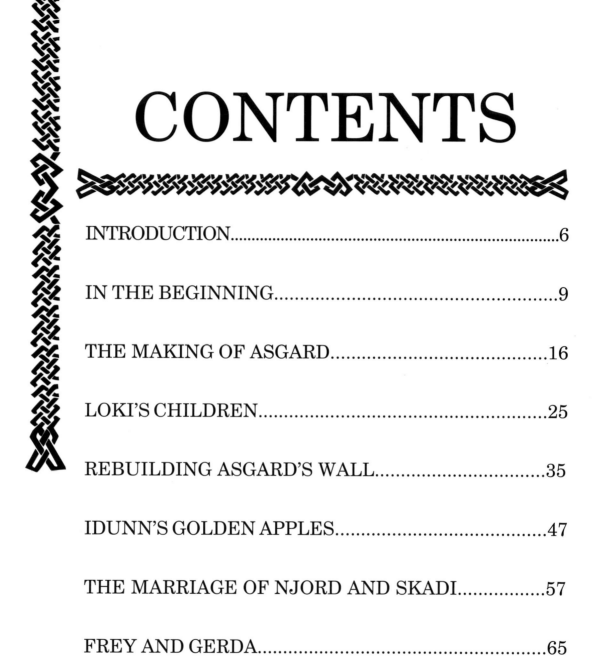

# INTRODUCTION

**H**ere are stories of gods and goddesses, sea monsters and ice giants, dark forests, flying chariots, shape-changers, cloud spinners and cunning, gold-hoarding underground dwarves. These are tales the Norsemen told to explain the way the world came into being and the powers that ruled it.

'Norsemen' means 'the people of the North', who lived in what we now call Norway, Sweden and Denmark more than 1500 years ago. They were a tough race. They had to be. They were farmers and traders, living in harsh climates where it was often a struggle to grow crops or rear animals. You needed plenty of land to yield enough grass to feed a flock of sheep and there came a time when there just wasn't enough land to go round.

Then the Norsemen put to good use their greatest skill of all. They were superb boat-builders and navigators, creating narrow, flexible ships that could safely ride rough seas. They had long been using these for trading and for raiding along their coastlines. When supplies were short, a raiding party was regarded as a very proper way of getting what you needed. It depended on daring, fearlessness and good leadership, qualities the Norsemen valued highly. A local chief would gather the best warriors from clans loyal to him and they would swoop down on a rival settlement and carry off everything of value they could get away with. There was a great deal of feasting afterwards to celebrate a good haul.

It was a short step from this sort of raid to thinking of raiding and seizing land overseas. This is what lay behind the sudden explosion of the pagan northerners who we now call the Vikings into more southerly, Christian Europe. For three hundred years, from the end of the 8th century, they plundered and laid waste, before finally settling and making their homes in France, in the Netherlands, in England, Ireland, the Orkneys, Iceland and Greenland.

Wherever they went, the Vikings took the tales of their pagan gods with them; not in written form, for few of them could read, but in their hearts. Families told and retold the old favourites around the fireside, and warriors feasting in their lord's hall were entertained with grander versions sung by professional poets. Luckily for us, the stories were gathered together and written down in Iceland around 1200. Thanks to this we can still listen to tales of the mysterious one-eyed Odin, lord of creation; of his hot-tempered son Thor, always looking for a fight with the hated ice giants; of Loki, the cunning trickster who loves to stir up trouble, and of the many other gods of Asgard, the golden land reached by the rainbow bridge. There's lots here to enjoy.

# IN THE BEGINNING

At the beginning of the world there were just two things – a realm of ice and snow called Niflheim and a realm of fire called Muspelheim. Muspelheim was ruled by the terrible fire giant Surtr. Between these two stretched Ginnungagap, a great emptiness, a yawning gap with nothing in it. Then suddenly, from a spring in the depth of Niflheim, eleven rivers bubbled up and streamed into the great gap, congealing into blocks of ice as they fell, so that in time the northern part of Ginnungagap was filled up and frozen solid. Where the hot sparks from

Muspelheim fell on this ice it began to thaw and to drip, and these drips contained life. As they fell they took the form of a sleeping giant. His name was Imir, and he was the first created being in the world.

Imir was an evil creature, the ancestor of the race of frost giants who later caused so much trouble to gods and men. While he slept, creatures, male and female, were born from the sweat of his armpits and one of his legs mated with the other to produce a son. This was how the first frost giants were fathered.

As more ice melted it took the form of a cow called Audumla. When Imir awoke from his sleep he drank the milk of the cow and grew huge and strong. Audumla, meanwhile, was licking the salt from the blocks of ice. She loved salt. She licked and licked and her warm tongue gradually melted the ice away. At the end of the first day she had uncovered the hair of a head. At the end of the second day she had licked the head free and the shoulders were appearing, and by the end of the third day she had uncovered a whole man from the ice. He was good and tall and handsome and powerful. This was Buri, the first ancestor of the gods. As time went on, Buri had a son called Bor who married a giant's daughter, Bestla. They had three sons, Vili, Ve, and the eldest and wisest of the three, who was named Odin.

Odin and his brothers refused to be bullied by Imir and his race of frost giants. The two families became sworn enemies. Odin led his brothers against the giants and killed Imir. So much blood spouted from his wounds that it formed a flood that drowned all the other giants except two, a rock giant and his wife. They got away in a make-shift boat and were carried on a tide of blood to the very edge of the world where their descendants created Giantland, the realm of the giants.

Meanwhile, Odin and his brothers dragged Imir's body to the middle of Ginnungagap and hacked it to pieces, and from these pieces they created the earth we know. They used Imir's bones to make its hills and mountains; his teeth to make its rocks and stones, his hair to make its grass and trees. The vast quantities of blood still flowing from the giant's wounds became the ocean, the lakes and the rivers.

After they had formed the earth, the brothers laid the ocean in a ring all around it. There was still no sky, so they heaved up Imir's skull to form a dome over the earth and commanded four dwarfs called North, South, East and West to hold the dome up at the corners of the world. The race of dwarfs had been born from the maggots that bred in Imir's flesh; they lived beneath the hills and mountains in caves deep underground. Then Odin tossed Imir's brains into the sky where they became the drifting clouds. He took sparks from Muspelheim and scattered them in the sky for stars, and from two especially large sparks he formed the sun and the moon and set them in golden chariots to light the sky. When the giants saw this they sent two wolves to devour them and bring back darkness. This is why the sun and the moon are always on the move across the sky. They are fleeing these hungry wolves. It is said that in the end the wolves will catch them, and that will signal the end of the world as we know it.

In this way the world was made and the earth grew green and flourishing, but there were still no people in it. Then, one day, Odin and his brothers were walking along the edge of the world where the earth meets the ocean, and they noticed that

the sea had washed up two fallen tree trunks worn smooth by the water. The brothers decided to make something of them. Odin breathed life into them, Vili gave them understanding and warm feelings, and Ve gave them hearing and sight – and so the first man and the first woman were made. The gods named the man Ash and the woman Elm. Then the brothers took Imir's bushy eyebrows and wove them into a strong fence which they set around the earth to keep the giants out. They called this safe place Midgard. Here they put Ash and Elm to live, and they were the ancestors of us all.

# THE MAKING OF ASGARD

**A**fter they had made the earth and sky, Odin and his brothers created their own realm called Asgard, a great stronghold full of shining palaces. They placed it high above Midgard and linked the two by a bridge called Bifrost, which was formed of the rainbow and was wondrously strong.

The whole of this newly-created world was supported by Yggdrasil, the World Ash, the largest and most stately of trees. Its branches spread out above the sky and overhung the worlds of men, of gods and of giants. This tree had existed for ever,

though it could not be seen by the eyes of ordinary beings. Without its support and protection the whole world would fall part.

The tree had three long roots. The first reached into Asgard, to the well of the Norns, the three mysterious sisters whose faces were always hidden in their grey shawls. They shaped the life and timed the death of every living being. Their well was especially holy. Each day the Norns took water from the well and sprinkled it upon the tree, so that its branches should never wither or rot.

The second root reached to the realm of the frost giants (where the Yawning Gap used to be). This was nourished by the well of Mimir, which was the source of all wisdom.

The third root sank into the depth of Niflheim, to a spring of icy waters that fed all the rivers of the world. A dragon gnawed constantly at this root, trying to destroy it, for evil beings were always looking for ways to harm the World Ash.

The Well of Mimir was named after the god who guarded it. He existed only as a head, but as he constantly drank from the well of wisdom it was the wisest head in the world. Odin made a special journey to taste the waters of this well so that he could become the master of all wisdom. When he asked to dip his drinking horn in its water he was told that such things must be paid for.

'How much must I pay?' Odin asked.

'You must give one of your eyes,' was the reply.

Odin valued the power of knowledge so much that without hesitating he tore out his right eye and flung it into the well. Then he filled his horn and drank, and so he gained his knowledge of the past, the present and the future. And it was for this reason that Odin, when he wandered the world in disguise as he sometimes liked to do, would pull a wide-brimmed hat well down over his eyes so that no one should spot his telltale empty eye socket.

Odin and his wife Frigg were the mother and father of all the gods, who honoured and obeyed them in everything. His palace in Asgard had a lofty tower which held his high throne from which he could look out over the whole wide world. Here he would often sit deep in thought with two ravens perched upon his shoulders. They were called Huginn (Thought) and Munin (Memory). Each day at dawn he sent them winging around the world, and when they returned they whispered in his ear every scrap of news they had heard during the day.

There were twelve chief gods among the followers of Odin and in their council chamber they sat on twelve thrones, with Odin presiding over them. Odin was a warrior god, fierce and frightening. Much more loveable, and a great favourite with the people of Midgard, was his eldest son, Thor, the thunder god. He was a huge rollicking red-

haired figure with a red beard and bushy red eyebrows who rumbled about the sky in a chariot drawn by two goats. He was enormously brave and strong but he was a bit short on brainpower. His favourite sport was giant hunting; his ambition was to rid the world entirely of these nasty creatures.

Odin's second son was Balder, the best, the kindest and fairest of all the gods, and loved by one and all (or all but one, as we shall see). Third amongst them was Tyr, the god of war, who was totally without fear, as he was soon to show. Then came kindly Njord who liked talk and good company. He ruled the winds and the oceans. Fishermen prayed to him for a good catch and sailors called for his help in stormy weather.

Njord had a son called Frey and a daughter called Freya, both favourites with the people of the earth. Frey had power over rain and sunshine and was the god of fruitfulness and peace. Freya was, quite simply, the most beautiful of all the goddesses, for she was the goddess of love.

The last of the gods of Asgard who must be named (though there were many others) was Heimdall, the watchman of the gods, who lived at the very edge of Asgard and guarded the Rainbow Bridge, always on the lookout for attack from ice giants or hill giants. He kept constant guard, sleeping with one eye open like a bird, and his ears were so keen that he could hear the noise of a blade of grass growing and the hairs getting longer on a sheep's back. As long as Heimdall was keeping watch, the gods knew Asgard was safe, and should he ever need to warn them of danger he had only to blow the great horn that hung at his side.

Now one name is missing from this list of gods, and that is because he really had no business to be there at all. Odin allowed him to come and go in Asgard, and it is said that in the past the two had sworn to be blood brothers – no one knew why. There must have been some bond between them for Odin to let such a troublemaker go free. His name was Loki and he was a liar and a mischief maker. Outwardly he was handsome and could be charming and a good companion, but inside he was full of spite and truly evil. He had such a gift for slyness that he could trick anyone into doing anything, and he often got the gods into hot water. Then, if they were lucky, he got them out again with some crafty advice. He has a big part to play in the stories of the gods.

# LOKI'S CHILDREN

**Y**ou never knew what to expect from Loki so the gods were not surprised to discover that, as well as a loving wife in Asgard, he had a secret wife in Giantland, an ogress named Angrboda, and that they were bringing up three horrible offspring together. Their firstborn was a savage wolf called Fenrir, the second a colossal serpent, and the third an evil-looking female called Hel. Looking into the future, Odin saw nothing but disaster for the gods if these three were allowed to grow up to do as they wished. He knew that at some time in the future, no one knew

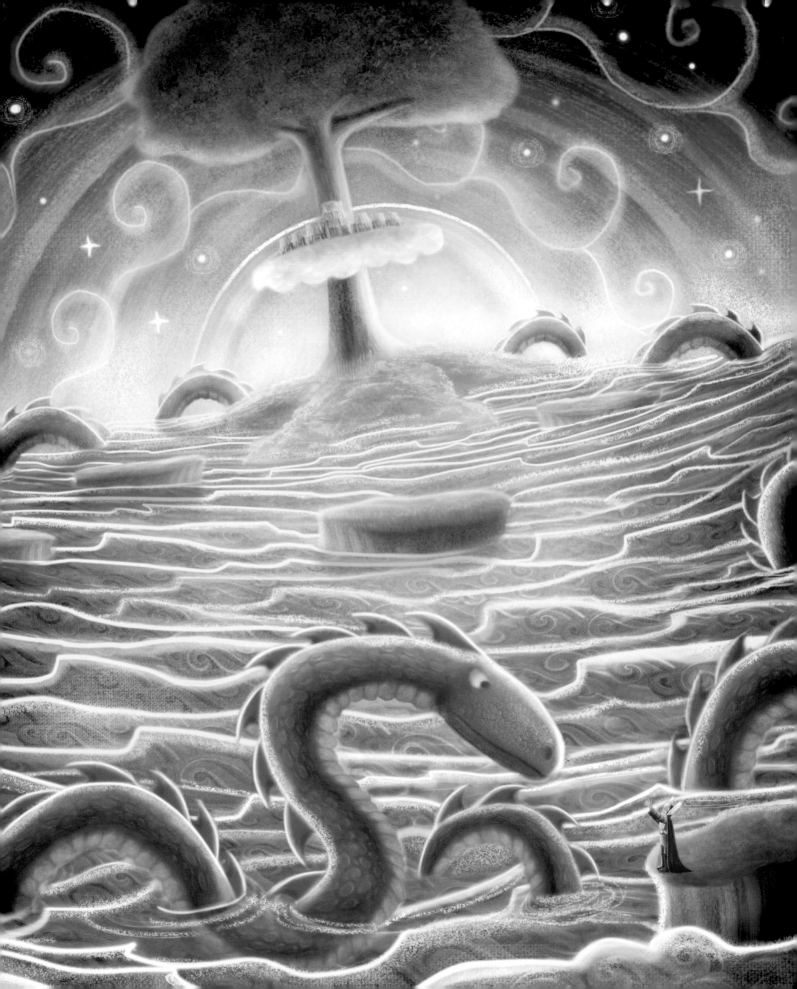

when, there would come the terrible day called Ragnarok, when the forces of good and evil would fight each other to the death. There was no doubt which side these creatures would be on.

Odin decided to imprison the young monsters before they got too powerful to control. He gave orders for them to be kidnapped and dragged before him. The serpent writhed its slimy body in coils so vast you could not see the end of them. 'I'll soon fix you,' cried Odin, and with one mighty heave he lifted the serpent high in the air and flung it into the sea beyond the shores of Giantland. There, it grew so huge that it wrapped itself around the whole world, till its head could grasp its tail in its mouth.

Next, Odin considered Hel. She was a chilling sight. From a distance she appeared to be a normal person, but if you took a closer look you saw that although the right side of her body was that of a beautiful woman, her left side was old and wrinkled and hideous. Even the two halves of her face were divided as if by a lightning strike. On the right side her face was pure, her eye shining and her hair lustrous and black. On the left she had the face of a corpse; the skin was blackish and the sunken eye was pitiless.

'You are no fit creature for this world,' said Odin, 'but I can find a job for you. You shall rule over the spirits of the dead. Not the noble spirits who have died a warrior's death in battle. They are welcomed in Asgard in my hall of heroes, called

Valhalla. You shall be queen of a frozen wasteland in the bottommost pits of Niflheim. There you will rule over the oath-breakers, the traitors and the murderers, and all those cowardly men who would rather die in their beds of old age than risk their

lives fighting for their lord. And we shall call your kingdom, Hel.'

Lastly, the gods discussed the fate of Fenrir. 'He is savage,' they agreed, 'but he is young. He can be trained. Let us have him in Asgard and keep an eye on him.' So the gods tried to treat Fenrir as a pet, until he grew so frighteningly large that no one except Tyr, who feared nothing, would go anywhere near him.

'We must tie him up,' the gods decided. They made a powerful chain of heavy iron links, but then no one wanted the job of putting it around Fenrir. Then Tyr had an idea. 'I've just been telling everyone how strong you are,' he told Fenrir. 'I'll put this chain around you and you can show how easily you can break it.'

Tyr wound the chain around Fenrir's neck and body and legs, and stood back to see what would happen. Fenrir planted his paws firmly, took a deep breath and flexed his muscles. The iron links split apart and the gods sprang back in fright.

The gods set to at once to forge another chain, this time twice as strong with links heavier than the heaviest anchor-chain. 'If you can break this,' said Tyr, 'you will be famous throughout the whole world as the strongest of all living creatures.'

Fenrir sniffed at the chain. He was not sure he could break it but he was too proud not to try. Once more he let Tyr bind him. He dug his claws into the earth, braced his legs and tightened his muscles until they were as hard as iron. He heaved and strained. Then, just as the gods thought they had him in their power, the chain burst.

'If anyone can make a chain that will not break,' Odin said, 'the dwarfs can.' He sent a messenger down into the deep caves under Midgard where the dwarfs lived and worked in darkness, making all manner of precious objects in their smithies and binding them with spells. 'Odin will pay you well,' they were told, and their eyes gleamed greedily. When the messenger returned he was carrying a fetter as slender, as smooth and as soft as a ribbon of silk.

'What's this!' cried Odin. 'Whatever is it made of?'

'Exactly what I asked,' said the messenger. 'They told me it is made of six things: the noise of a cat's footfall, a woman's beard, the roots of a mountain, the nerves of a bear, the breath of a fish and a bird's spittle.'

'I suppose we must trust the dwarfs,' said Odin, doubtfully, running the silky binding through his fingers. 'Fenrir will make short work of that,' said the other gods, though when they tried to themselves they were not so sure.

Once again the gods came to Fenrir and Tir stepped forward and showed him the dwarf's fetter. Fenrir looked at it and snarled, baring his incredibly sharp teeth. 'This is some trick,' he growled. You don't catch me that way! There's more to this than just a bit of ribbon and I'm not letting you wind it around me.'

'There's no trick at all,' Tyr assured him. 'It's true it's stronger than it looks but you'll be sure to break it. And if you can't we'll know that you're not nearly as strong as we thought you were, and we'll set you free.'

'Huh!' said Fenrir. 'I'd be a fool to believe that.'

'Trust me,' said Tyr.

'I'll show how far I trust the lot of you,' said Fenrir. 'I need a guarantee you won't double-cross me. I'll only let you tie that thing around me if, all the time you're doing it, one of you puts his right hand into my mouth and keeps it there.'

The gods looked at each other. No one volunteered. It looked like a sure way of losing your right hand. Then Tyr stepped forward and put his hand between the wolf's jaws.

So the gods bound Fenrir with the dwarfs' slender fetter. They tied it around his throat, across his chest, between his legs and around his haunches, and bound his forefeet together with it. When he tried to flex his muscles the bond tightened around him, and the more he struggled the tighter it grew. The gods saw that he was helpless at last and they laughed and cheered with relief – all except Tyr who had his hand bitten off.

The gods passed the end of the dwarfs' fetter through a hole in a huge rock, looped it back and tied it to itself. Then they hammered the rock down into the earth and dropped a giant boulder on top to hold it fast. All this while, Fenrir was lunging and snapping at everyone with his razor sharp jaws, so Odin took a sword and wedged his mouth open. He jammed the point into the wolf's bottom jaw and forced the pommel up against the roof of his mouth. That stopped him biting!

The gods thought that they had defeated Loki's evil children. Only Odin knew that they were waiting till the day of Ragnarok, when they would be set free once again.

# REBUILDING ASGARD'S WALL

**I**n a great battle between the gods and the giants the wall around Asgard had been almost entirely destroyed. Nothing was left but a ring of rubble. All the gods agreed that the wall ought to be rebuilt to prevent another attack, but no one was eager to take on the job. Then one day Heimdall the watchman saw a solitary rider on a black horse coming towards him over the rainbow bridge. Hel challenged the stranger to state his reason for coming to Asgard. The horseman replied that he was here to put a business plan to the gods and wanted to speak directly to Odin. So all the gods and goddesses gathered in their great hall, Gladsheim, to hear what the stranger had to say.

'Tell us what you propose,' said Odin, fixing him with his one eye.

'Just this,' replied the stranger. 'I'm a builder, a master mason. I can rebuild Asgard's wall for you. I'll make it stronger and higher than before. Much stronger and much higher. The ice giants and the hill trolls will never be able to break through it.'

'And what do you want in return?' asked Odin.

'I need eighteen months,' said the stranger. 'I can't do it in less.'

'You know that's not what I mean,' said Odin sharply. 'What do you hope to be paid?'

'I want Freya as my wife,' said the builder, as if this was the most reasonable thing in the world. At this there was a great gasp from the gods. How dare he ask such a thing! Freya, goddess of love, was the most beautiful of all the goddesses and the most beloved by gods and humankind. As if she could be given away to any old stranger who came to the door!

'Yes, I'll have Freya, and I want the sun and the moon too,' said the builder. 'That's my price.'

At this there was uproar in the hall. The gods began shouting and waving their fists at the builder and demanding that he be kicked out.

Then Loki's voice was heard amidst the hubbub. 'Let's not be too hasty. There may be something in this plan, if we can work out a compromise.'

There was a hush while everybody took this in. Most of the gods were suspicious of any plan of Loki's, and Freya's face showed plainly that any sort of discussion would be an insult to her. Odin looked thoughtful and said that in courtesy to their visitor the gods would consider the matter – in private.

When the builder had left the hall Loki explained his plan. 'Suppose we say that he must do the work in six months.'

'Impossible,' said someone. 'He'd never manage it.'

'Exactly! But even if he only managed half of it we'd still have half a wall for nothing. We wouldn't have to pay him if he didn't finish in the time agreed. Of course he may refuse our terms, but we've got nothing to lose by asking.'

The gods felt uneasy about taking Loki's advice but they couldn't see anything wrong with it. Odin called the builder back and told him their decision. 'We'll let you have six months for the job. Tomorrow is the first day of winter and if every part of the wall is finished by the first day of summer Freya shall be yours and you will get the sun and the moon thrown in. But if you don't finish in time you will not be paid. Is that agreed?'

'That's impossible,' said the builder. 'I'd need help.'

'No help at all,' said Odin. 'You must do the work entirely by yourself.'

'At least allow me to use my horse Svadilfari.'

'No help means no help. Take it or leave it,' replied Odin.

'Oh, let him have his horse,' exclaimed Loki. 'It can't make any difference. Otherwise there'll be no bargain and we shan't get any wall at all.'

So in the end it was agreed. The bargain was made before witnesses and confirmed with solemn oaths. The next morning, before it was even daylight, the builder started work. Or rather, Svadilfari started, for it was astonishing to see what a weight of stone that horse could haul from the quarry. He heaved and strained throughout the hours of darkness, so that by dawn there was enough stone stacked at the building site to keep the mason at work non-stop till it was night again. The gods looked on with alarm as the wall began

rapidly taking shape. By the time spring came Asgard was almost encircled by a wall of well-cut stone, and at this rate the builder would soon be sending in his bill. Freya was shedding pools of tears. When only three days were left before the start of summer, Odin called a meeting to discuss the crisis. Everyone was looking for someone to blame. 'How did we get into this fix?' they were asking, and everyone looked at Loki. Odin strode across the hall and stood towering over him. 'This was your idea. You suggested this bargain. Now get us out of it.'

'But it isn't my fault. We all agreed.'

'And who suggested we should let him use his horse? You did, Loki. So you start thinking hard, because if you don't get us out of this mess you'll pay for it with your life.'

Loki was really frightened. He saw that Odin meant what he said and all the other gods were looking at him menacingly. 'No need to worry.

None at all. I'll manage something,' he promised. 'Just you wait and see.'

Now Loki was a shape changer. He could transform himself into anything he wished, so when the gods noticed he had vanished they knew that he was up to one of his tricks. The next morning, just as the builder was harnessing Svadilfari to draw up the day's quota of stone, the prettiest-looking little grey mare came skipping out of the woods. She pranced up to Svadilfari and whinnied invitingly. Then she danced off into the woods again. The huge black horse strained so hard to follow her that he snapped the traces that held him and disappeared after her into the trees. The builder ran after them shouting and cursing, but though he searched the woods all day he could find no sign of his horse. Without Svadilfari he could not shift the stone, so no work was done upon the wall that day.

The next day was just the same. Though the builder called and called to Svadilfari the horse had better things to do and would not show himself. By the last day of spring the builder was in a towering rage. 'You've snared my horse! You've cheated me!' he stormed. 'I'll smash you all to smithereens.' In his fury he burst out of his disguise and showed himself in his true shape, a horrible rock giant. 'We don't do business with giants,' the gods declared. 'Get out of here!'

But the rock giant would not leave and vowed he would have vengeance on them. Then Thor lost

his patience and brought his hammer, Mjolnir, crashing down on the giant's skull which broke into a thousand pieces. That was the end of him.

So the gods got a fine wall built for nothing. They only had to finish its gateway. Loki meanwhile had vanished, but some months later he came sauntering over the rainbow bridge, bringing a young grey colt along with him. It was a fine animal although there was certainly something odd about it. It had eight legs!

'This is for you,' said Loki to Odin. 'A peace offering after the spot of trouble we had. It's my very own child I'm giving you, born while I was a mare. You'll never find a horse to match it for strength or swiftness, I promise you.'

Odin was pleased with the gift. He called the horse Sleipnir, and although Loki's promises were usually not worth much, in this case he spoke true. No creature could outpace Odin's fabulous eight-legged horse.

# IDUNN'S GOLDEN APPLES

O n a tree in a forest in Asgard grew the golden apples of immortality. The tree was cared for by the gentle goddess Idunn. Only she knew where it was. She harvested the apples and placed them in an ash-wood casket, and from time to time she gave each god an apple from her casket to eat. The apples gave them youth and strength so that they never grew old.

It happened one day that Odin and his brother Hoenir, full of the energy of Idunn's apples, decided to spend a day walking through the wilder parts of Midgard to see how the people there were getting on.

'I'll come with you,' said Loki, who didn't want to miss the chance of learning something that he might find useful.

So the three of them set off early and wandered all day through isolated villages and farms. It was getting on for evening when they realised they were hungry and had brought no food with them. They were on a barren hillside and could see no dwelling anywhere that could offer hospitality. Then Odin's keen eye spotted a fold in the hills that proved to shelter a little grassy valley where cattle were grazing. They cornered a fat ox and killed it and got a fire going, chopping the meat into joints and burying it in the hot embers to roast. Then they sat around the fire impatiently with their stomachs rumbling.

'Loki, take a look and see if it's done,' said Odin after a while. Loki kicked the embers aside with his boot and prodded the meat. 'It seems to need a good deal yet,' he said and he heaped the embers over it again.

So the gods sat and waited and could think of nothing but getting their teeth into that juicy meat. They allowed enough time for even the largest pieces to be done but when they tested it again it was still almost raw.

'This is not natural,' said Odin. 'There is some power here that is working against us.'

'The meat will not be cooked until I say it will,' said a hoarse voice from above their heads. The gods looked up and saw a huge eagle sitting on the topmost branch of an oak tree near the fire. 'The cattle are mine and the meat is mine, and it will not be cooked unless you let me be the first to eat from it.'

The gods were in no position to refuse. 'Please be our guest,' they said.

The eagle spread its huge wings and with a rattling of feathers it swooped down on the fire and pulled out a big shoulder joint, tore at the flesh with its beak and had eaten it to the bone in an instant. He set about the rest of the meat with the same speed. 'He'll have the lot if we don't stop him!' yelled Loki, and seizing a stout stick he began to beat the eagle off. The eagle gave a furious screech and rose into the air, taking Loki with him, for however hard Loki tried he found that he could not let go of the stick. Up, up the eagle rose into the air, with Loki dangling and shouting for help. He thought that the bird meant to drop him from a great height but apparently it had something more amusing in mind. It came down almost to the ground and skimmed along at just the right level to bash Loki's shins and knee-caps against the rocks and rip his flesh on the thorn bushes. Still Loki could not let go though he thought his arms would be pulled from their sockets.

'Who are you and what do you want from me?' cried Loki. 'I'll give you anything if you let me go.'

'I am Thiazzi the storm giant and I wish to be immortal like the gods. If you promise me that in three days time you will bring me Idunn and her apples I will set you free.'

'I will! I will! I promise you!' swore Loki.

Then Loki's hands were free and he tumbled to the ground. The eagle flew off and Loki hobbled back to his comrades, though he did not mention the promise he had made.

Three days later Loki came to Idunn and told her he had something wonderful to show her. 'It's a tree in a forest in Midgard which bears golden apples just like yours.'

'You can't be right,' said Idunn. 'No tree in the world has apples like mine.'

'These are the same, I swear it! Come and have a look. And bring your apples with you so that we can compare the two.'

Trusting Idunn went down into Midgard with Loki, carrying her casket of apples, and there Thiazzi in his eagle form swooped down on her and carried her back to Jotunheim.

It took the gods some time to realise that Idunn was missing, but when they did they grew very anxious. They knew that without the juicy freshness of her apples they would soon grow old. In fact some of them were looking rather withered already. There was a streak of grey in Freya's hair and wrinkles round her eyes; Heimdall's wonderful eyesight was not as sharp as it used to be and Odin's joints were beginning to creak.

An emergency meeting was called to discuss the crisis, and it was established that Idunn had last been seen walking down the rainbow bridge with Loki by her side. Then Loki was dragged out and forced to confess. In their fury the gods threatened him with torture and death unless he went to Jotunheim and brought back Idunn and her casket of apples.

Loki saw he had no choice. 'If Freya will lend me her falcon-skin cloak I'll soon bring Idunn back,' he boasted, though inwardly he was not so sure. With the cloak on his back he became a falcon and winged with all speed to distant Giantland. He reached its dreary mountains and bleak coast and came to Thiazzi's castle on a headland overlooking the sea. Loki's luck was in. He could see Thiazzi in a fishing boat some distance out to sea and his daughter Skadi was with him. Loki found poor Idunn huddled in a chilly room, clasping her

apples to her chest. He swiftly transformed her into a nut, which he seized in his claws before flying off as fast as he could.

When Thiazzi and his daughter brought home their catch and found Idunn was gone, the giant flew into a rage and cursed the gods of Asgard. He was sure they were behind it all. He put on his eagle-skin and set off to catch the culprit. The distance between Jotunheim and Asgard was great but the eagle was much stronger than the falcon. As Loki neared the wall of Asgard the eagle had almost caught up with him. Then, at Odin's command, the gods gathered bins of wood shavings from the carpenter's shop and tipped them in a pile before the wall. As Loki, at his last gasp, flung himself over the wall to safety, the gods set a torch to the shavings which exploded into flame. The eagle was so close behind that he could not stop in time. The flames turned his skin to cinders so that he fell to the ground right in the gateway to Asgard. There the gods with their swords put a quick end to the giant Thiazzi.

Idunn opened her casket and gave everyone an apple so that that they were quickly young again. Loki snatched his and hurried away. The Mischief Maker thought he'd better keep out of sight until the part he'd played in Idunn's kidnap was safely forgotten.

# THE MARRIAGE OF NJORD AND SKADI

While the gods were celebrating the death of Thiazzi the storm giant, his daughter Skadi strode up and down on the headland in Giantland, anxiously waiting for him to come home. When news reached her that he was dead, slain by the gods of Asgard, she was overcome with grief, for she had loved her father dearly. But her sorrow soon changed to fury and she swore vengeance on his murderers.

Skadi went to her father's armoury and put on a tunic of chain mail, a helmet, shield and a spear, and buckled on his finest sword. Then she set out fearlessly for Asgard.

Heimdall saw this warlike figure approaching over Bifrost and warned the gods that the giant's daughter was coming in no friendly mood. But Odin had no wish to start a feud that might bring all the giants to attack Asgard. He persuaded the gods to offer Skadi compensation for her father's death. They agreed to pay her gold.

Skadi treated the idea with scorn. 'You burn my father alive and then you offer me gold? My father's coffers are full of gold. I do not need your gold!'

'Then what would satisfy you?' asked Odin. 'If it is anything possible you shall have it.'

'I want a husband,' said Skadi. 'A husband who is a god. I want one of you to marry me.'

There was a stunned silence. No one volunteered to be the bridegroom.

'We will discuss this matter among ourselves,' said Odin, leading the way to the council chamber. 'A promise is a promise,' he told the assembled gods. 'If none of you will offer to marry her we must let her choose a husband. But we'll make it hard for her to cherry-pick the best.'

Skadi was told that she could choose any of the gods to be her husband, but she must do so from the look of their bare feet. The gods lined up behind a partition that didn't quite reach to the ground and Skadi took a good look at each pair of feet. She knew what she was looking for. She wanted Baldur, nicknamed the Beautiful because he was the handsomest of all the gods. Everything about him was attractive, so surely his feet would be the cleanest and freshest of them all. These were the feet that Skadi chose, but they proved to belong to Njord, the god of seafarers and fishing. His feet were spotless from so much wading in the sea.

Skadi did nothing to hide her disappointment but Njord, who was a good-hearted, cheery person,

was quite ready to make the best of the marriage forced upon him. 'We'll have good times together,' he said, giving the giant's daughter an encouraging hug. She looked doubtful and despondent.

'Where shall we live?' she asked. 'I hate the sea. I could not bear to leave my frozen mountains. I love the glaciers, the ice-bound lakes and the wind that roars through the valleys. I want to have my snow-shoes on my feet to skim about as freely as I like. I could not sit upon a beach and wait around for you.'

'I'll love those mountains too, for your sake,' Njord replied. So it was agreed that they should begin their married life in Skadi's castle, Thrymheim ('thunder-home'), high in the mountains where the snow never melts. Njord found the castle dark and draughty. He stamped around its rooms trying to keep his feet warm, or huddled close to the fire. Skadi never felt the cold so the fire was not a big one. It warmed Njord's chest but not his back, so he had to pile on layers of cloaks. Skadi was out all day hunting gazelles and mountain foxes but Njord was too numb with cold to feel like joining her. At night Skadi slept like a log but Njord lay listening to the wind and the howling of the wolves, and got scarcely a wink of sleep.

After nine days of this Njord could bear it no more. 'I think I must take a look at my shipyards back home,' he told Skadi. 'I need to keep an eye on things, you know. Why don't you come with

me? You might like life by the sea much more than you think. It's busy and bright and everyone's friendly.' Skadi looked doubtful but at least she agreed to try it.

How glad Njord was to smell the salt air again, to hear the cries of the gulls and the soothing sound of the waves breaking on the beach. His home was right on the shore, overlooking the harbour which was crowded with fishing boats and big square-sailed merchant ships. You could tell from the shouts of welcome that Njord was a favourite with all the sea-going folk.

'Come and see the fine long-ship they're working on at the moment,' he called to Skadi. He took her to the shipyard where carpenters were hammering home a ship's long timbers with iron nails. 'It'll be due for launching soon and then we'll have a great feast to give it a send off,' he told her, grinning at the thought. But Skadi was not smiling. The noise of the hammering, the chiselling and the sawing made her head ache.

'I can't bear all this banging and shouting,' she said. 'And all those screaming gulls – they won't let me get to sleep at night. I know you love your boats but you're not going to get me into one. Never!'

So, sadly, Njord and Skadi decided that although they were fond of one another they would have to live apart. Skadi returned to her mountains where she could draw deep breaths of the icy air that she had missed; Njord stayed with the seafarers who loved and needed him. But if ever chance brought them together they were always very glad to see each other.

# FREY AND GERDA

**F**rey and his sister Freya were the favourite gods of the people of Midgard, for most of them were farmers and these were the gods that cared for everything that grows. Wherever they went, plants flourished, crops ripened, farm animals thrived and were fertile and young people fell in love.

As far as love was concerned, Frey left that sort of thing to his sister, for he had never been in love. Perhaps he never would have been were it not for the fact that Frey was mischievous –

too mischievous for his own good. One day he accompanied his father, Njord, to Odin's palace to a business conference to which all the gods had been summoned. That sort of thing didn't interest Frey at all. He liked adventure. He decided to slip away and do some exploring on his own.

Wandering round the palace he came to the stairway that led to the watch tower that housed Odin's high seat. Frey knew that when the king of the gods sat in this seat he was able to see everything that went on in the world. Frey didn't hesitate. He ran up the stairs, opened the heavy oak door at the top and climbed into the seat. All these things were strictly forbidden. Huggin and Munin thrust out their necks and rattled their feathers at him but he didn't care. He found that he could see beyond Asgard, beyond Midgard, right as far as the land of the Giants, and even beyond that, to the sea at the end of the world. He imagined himself king of all these realms. It was a great game.

As he was gazing out over Giantland, Frey saw a fine city there, and within it a very splendid house which he recognised as the home of Gymir, one of the fiercest of the mountain giants. As Frey watched, a beautiful young woman came walking towards the house. This was Gerda, the Giant's daughter, for you must know that not all the offspring of giants are hideous. Far from it. As Gerda raised her hands to unlatch the door a most beautiful light shone from them that lit up the whole of the earth, the sky and the sea.

Frey felt a pang throughout his whole being. He knew he could not live without such beauty. Gerda must be his wife. Yet he knew she never could be. Gymir would never let his daughter marry one of the gods of Asgard, his most hated enemies. Frey staggered down Odin's stairway, sick at heart, and when he got home he shut himself up in his palace and would not speak to anyone.

Very soon the gods became worried. Frey would not say what was wrong with him. He moped all

day and every day, and gave no thought to tending the growing things that relied on him. If nothing was done soon the crops would all be blighted and the cattle starved. Njord demanded an explanation from his son but Frey would not answer him. In despair Njord summoned Skirnir, Frey's faithful servant. The two had grown up together and used to be playmates. 'Go to my son,' said Njord. 'If he will tell anyone his troubles it will be to you.'

Skirnir found Frey lying on his bed with his head buried in his arms. He would not even turn to look at his old friend. Skirnir reminded him how they had always shared each other's secrets. 'This is different,' Frey replied. 'This is serious – deadly.'

'No one can help you if you don't say what is wrong,' said Skirnir.

'And no one can help me if I do,' moaned Fry. 'I know that Odin and every god in Asgard will be against me – even my dear sister Freya will no longer love me.'

'Nonsense,' said Skirnir. 'It cannot be as bad as that.'

'I tell you it is the worst thing possible!' cried Frey. 'I am dying, yes, dying for love of Gymir's daughter Gerda, and her father will never let me have her. He is asking the impossible. He will only let me marry her if I give him the sword the light elves made for me.'

Skirnir's mouth dropped open with horror. Frey's sword was a magic weapon forged especially for him by the elves. It had the gift of being able to fight by itself and it could never be defeated. The gods would need it on the day of Ragnarok to do battle with the giants. It was for that very reason that the elves had forged it with such powerful spells and had given it to Frey.

'But I must have Gerda!' cried Frey suddenly, leaping up. 'Take my sword, Skirnir, give it to Thrym and bring her to me.'

'But even if I took your sword I couldn't enter Gymir's stronghold,' objected Skirnir. 'You know as well as I do that it's fenced around by barriers of flame that no one can pass through.'

'If they can't pass through they can leap over,' said Frey, now in a frenzy of impatience. 'Borrow Odin's eight-legged horse. He will carry you over easily. Go now I beg you, while Odin is asleep.'

Skirnir felt his breath knocked right out of him by the dreadfulness of what Frey was asking. Steal the wondrous horse of the king of the gods, ride it to Giantland and make it leap over sheets of flame, just to fix up a marriage that everyone would hate! But he loved his master and felt he must obey, though secretly he was determined not to give up the sword. He crept silently into the royal stables, saddled Sleipnir and galloped out through the night air to Giantland.

A wall of fire, blazing in the night sky, guided Skirnir to his goal. When Sleipnir reached the flames he did not falter but launched himself forward and upward wth a mighty leap. Then horse and rider landed safely in the giant's courtyard. Thrym, the giant, was waiting for them.

'Who are you and what do you want, little skinny-shanks?' he roared.

'I am a messenger from the great god Frey,' Skirnir answered boldly. 'I have good news for you. That

young and handsome and glorious god would like your daughter, Gerda, to be his bride.'

Thrym gave a great mocking laugh at this, but Gerda opened her chamber window and leaned out to learn more. 'What can Frey offer as a dowry?' she asked.

'He offers eleven golden apples from Idunn's basket. They will keep your beauty fresh for ever.'

'I do not want your apples. I have no need of them,' said Gerda.

'He will give you a golden ring which will produce eight more rings every ninth night.'

'I do not want his gold. I have chests full of gold,' said Gerda. 'But offers always come in threes. What is Frey's third offer?'

Still brave Skirnir was not willing to name Frey's sword. Instead he tried to frighten Gerda: if she

would not agree he would strike off her head.
Gerda just laughed. 'My father will protect me.
You would be dead before you had time to draw
your blade.'

Then Skirnir threatened Gerda with the most
terrible curses that he could think of. He would
force her to live forever on the threshold of Hel,
without hope of escape. All her food would be
loathsome to her and she would be forced to drink
the urine of goats. He told her she would suffer
rage, longing, fetters, wrath, tears and torment. She would dwell forever with three-headed giants and have no other husband. Her beauty would shrivel like a dried up thistle. All this he would bind upon her through the power of the

magic writing known as runes. 'But if you agree to marry Frey I can unwrite these runes,' said Skirnir.

'I do not fear your threats,' said Gerda. 'Name your third offer.'

'He knows our price. He is wasting our time,' snarled Thrym.

Then Skirnir knew he was defeated and handed over Frey's magic sword.

So Gerda came to Asgard to be Frey's bride. Odin forgave them and they were happy together. And Thrym, now he had the sword, gave no more trouble for quite a while.

But on the day of Ragnarok Frey felt the lack of the sword most bitterly, and wished a thousand times he had not given it away.

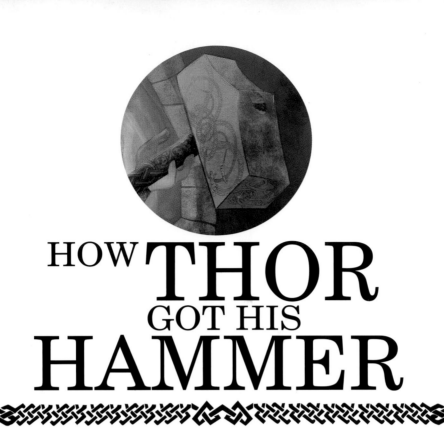

# HOW THOR GOT HIS HAMMER

**S**if, the wife of Thor the thunder god, had the most beautiful hair. It fell over her shoulders and down her back in ripples of gold and she was very proud of it. Now one day Loki, who was mischievous in his good moods and evil in his bad ones, decided it would be a great joke to cut off Sif's hair. He crept into her bedroom while she slept and cut it all off at the roots, leaving her as bald as a dandelion clock when you have puffed off all the seeds. Thor was away giant hunting but when he got back the next day he found his home in an uproar. Sif was screeching and sobbing, and

her attendants who were trying to calm her were making matters worse.

'Who's done this to you?' roared Thor. 'Who's dared to touch my wife's head and make it look like a pig's bladder?'

At this Sif bellowed all the louder. 'It's Loki for sure. It's just the sort of spiteful thing he'd do,' she wailed.

'Wait till I get my hands on him! I'll break every bone in his body,' Thor swore. And he set about it right away, found Loki's hiding place, shook him by the neck and swung him around in the air till his brains rattled.

'Where's your sense of humour? You know I'll put it right,' Loki gasped. 'I'll get Sif new hair of pure gold. If I can't no one can,' he added cunningly. So Thor grudgingly let Loki go, on his promise to bring Sif new hair by the end of the day.

Loki went at once to the realm of the dwarfs, the dark underground caverns where they forged tools and weapons and jewellery with a skill that even the gods could not equal. It was said that the greatest craftsmen of them all were two dwarfs known as the sons of Ivaldi, and it was to their smithy that Loki picked his way through the dark tunnels. 'Can you make me a cap of hair, all of the finest gold, that will grow on the head of the wearer like real hair?' he asked them.

'Nothing easier,' said the brothers. They set to work at once. They stoked up the furnace in the smithy and blew on its fire with the bellows to fan it into a blaze. When it had reached a fine heat they put in some lengths of gold wire and worked the bellows non-stop to keep up the blaze. When they opened the furnace again they drew out a cap of hair like silken gold that hung in heavy waves, yet every strand was so light the air could ruffle it.

'Wonderful,' said Loki. 'Sif's own hair was never so thick and fine.'

'You had better take a gift for Odin too, and one for Frey, or they may think we do not honour the gods of Asgard equally,' said the brothers.

'As you wish,' said Loki. 'What do you suggest?'

'Wait and see,' they replied. They returned to the smithy and Loki heard a frenzy of sawing and hammering and muttering of spells. Then one of the brothers came out bearing a magnificent spear with a mighty ashwood shaft banded with silver, and an iron head with a pattern like swirling flames. 'This is for Odin,' he said. 'It is called Gungnir. Tell him it will never falter in its flight or miss its aim.'

Then the second brother showed Loki a tiny ship, no bigger than a child's hand. 'This is for Frey,' he said. 'Its name is Skidbladnir. Tell him that it is not a toy but a real ship folded small for easy carrying. When he wishes to sail it will grow big enough to carry all the gods and it will always have a fair wind to speed it along wherever it needs to go.'

Loki thanked the dwarfs warmly and, bundling up the three gifts in his arms, set off for the daylight. But he must have taken a wrong turning in the rocky corridors for he passed the entrance to a smithy that was quite unknown to him. A burly dwarf with a knobbly face looked out at him.

'Who are you and what's that stuff you're carrying?' he demanded disagreeably.

'This "stuff" as you call it is a gift for the gods of Asgard, made by the finest craftsmen in the world.'

'And who are these fine craftsmen?'

'The sons of Ivaldi, of course. I live among the gods and know such things. My name is Loki.'

'Well my names's Brokk, and I can tell you, Loki Know-all, that you are wrong. My brother Sindri can make far finer treasures than Ivaldi's sons.'

'Liar!' said Loki. 'I'd like to see him try. I'm willing

to wager my head that he can't make anything to match the gifts I'm carrying.'

'Your head against mine then that my brother can make gifts that put the sons of Ivaldi right in the shade. We'll have a competition and let the gods decide whose work is better.'

Loki had to agree or lose face entirely. 'This Brokk is just a boaster,' he told himself. 'I'm sure to win.'

Brokk went into the smithy to explain the wager to his brother, who seemed to think there was no danger of Brokk losing his head. 'If you keep the bellows going,' said Sindri, 'you can rely on me for the rest.' Loki, lurking in the shadows, was really worried when he heard this. He must make sure the firing went wrong.

Sindri put hammered gold into the furnace and laid a pigskin on the roaring fire. 'Keep up the work with the bellows,' he told his brother. 'Never stop for a minute or my work will be spoilt.'

Quick as a pig blinks Loki changed himself into a horsefly and bit Brokk's leathery hand as hard as he could. But Brokk barely felt the bite and went on pumping, so that when Sindri opened the furnace his work was perfect – a living boar with bristles of gold that shone with light.

Next, Sindri took a lump of molten gold and hammered it into a ring and placed it in the furnace. 'Keep pumping,' he warned. This time Loki settled on Brokk's neck and bit him twice as hard, but Brokk just shook his head a bit and went on pumping. When Sindri opened the furnace he drew out a heavy gold arm band and Loki saw that it was perfect.

Next, Sindri heated a great lump of iron. He hammered it into a shape, hammered it again and reshaped it and went on hammering until he was satisfied. 'This will be a fine piece,' he said as he put it in the furnace for firing. 'But keep pumping, Brokk. It will be wrecked if the bellows stop.'

This time Loki settled on Brokk's forehead and stung him so hard that the blood ran down into his eye and he could not see. He put up a hand to wipe it away and for that one second the bellows were not pumping. Sindri came to open the furnace and drew out a huge battle hammer. When he examined it he found the handle was rather too short because of the moment when the bellows stopped. 'It is a mighty weapon all the same,' he said and handed the three gifts to Brokk to take to Asgard for the gods to judge.

Loki and Brokk produced their gifts before the gods in their council chamber. To Odin, Loki gave the spear, explaining its magic properties, and the king of the gods was very pleased with it. Frey was entranced by the amazing boat and Thor, of course, got the hair. He set it on Sif's head and at once it rooted like her own hair only, if possible, even more beautiful. She was wild with delight and rushed off to find a mirror.

Then Brock stepped forward, offering first to Odin the gold arm ring. 'This ring is called Draupnir,' he said. Every ninth night eight more gold rings will fall from it, bringing you constant wealth. For you, Frey, I bring Gullinbursti, the boar with the golden bristles. Never again will you travel in darkness, for the light from his bristles will show you the way. And he will carry you across sea and sky faster than any horse.

Then Brokk took the mighty battle axe and gave it to Thor. 'This is Miollnir,' he said. 'When it is thrown it will never miss its target and it will always return to your hand. With this weapon and your strength, Thor, the gods will be well protected.'

With all these wonders to choose from the gods took time to decide, but finally they declared the hammer was the best of the treasures as it was the finest defence against the giants. So Sindri was declared the winner and Loki's head was due to be cut off. But Loki had been doing some quick thinking. 'You can have my head, Brokk,' he said, 'but take care not to injure my neck. That was no part of the bargain.'

The gods laughed and said it was a fair point. 'Well at least I can do what I like with his head,' said a very disgruntled Brokk. And he pierced a series of holes round Loki's lips and sewed them up with a leather thong. It was quite a few days before Loki managed to pull out the stitches and talk again, and the gods agreed that these were the most restful days they had ever known.

# GLOSSARY

**Ancestor**
A person or people who lived in the past and from whom other people have descended.

**Fetter**
Bonds or chains used to restrain someone and prevent them from moving freely.

**Furnace**
A container in which materials like metal can be heated to very high temperatures for moulding.

**Iceland**
An island country between North America and Europe in the North Atlantic Ocean. It was first occupied by the Vikings.

**Immortality**
The supernatural ability to live forever without dying of old age or illness.

**Pommel**
The knob on the end of a sword's handle.

**Quarry**
A large pit where rock has been removed from the ground for use in building work.

**Raven**
A large type of crow with black feathers.

**Smithy**
The workshop where a blacksmith forges metal tools or weapons.

**Valhalla**
In Viking mythology, this is the afterlife for warriors who die heroically in battle. It's a great hall where food and drink are served and the warriors can fight each other for entertainment.